# CAP IT OFF WITH A SMILE

## A Guide for Making Friends

written and illustrated by

## Robin Inwald, Ph.D.

 **HILSON PRESS**
A division of Hilson Research, Inc.

LIBRARY OF CONGRESS CATALOG CARD NUMBER: 94-77395

Inwald, Robin.
Cap it off with a smile / by Robin Inwald, Ph.D.

Summary:  Using the letters C-A-P-S, children learn how  they can
make friends.

ISBN 1-885738-00-5 Cloth Edition     ISBN 1-885738-01-3  Paperbound Edition

 1. How to make friends - Juvenile literature.  2. Self-help.

For my son Michael

Sometimes it feels as if
Nothing is working out right...
You stay up and worry
About it at night.

Friends pick on you
And you don't know why.
They make fun of you often.
You try not to cry.
Everyone at school seems
To have a best friend.
You feel like the teammate
Who's picked at the end.

The class chooses you
As the one to tease,
And even the teacher
Is hard to please.

You try not to notice.
You say you don't care,
But deep down inside
A hurt feeling is there.
It's that they don't like you.
They've said it as well.
A plan just for you
Is what I'll now tell.

Stop a minute to think.
This can all go away
If you follow four rules
That I will now say.
Making friends is not easy.
It takes certain skill.
Listen now as I tell you,
For tell you I will!

The main word is CAP,
Like the one on my head,
To keep in the cold words
And spread warmth instead.

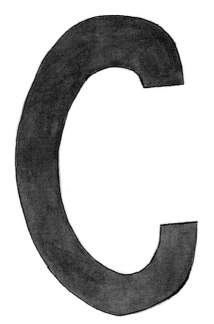

The first letter is C
And it means COMPLIMENT.
When you say someone looks nice,
It's time very well spent.
I don't mean you should lie
Or say something untrue,
Like, "I think you look great"
When your friend has the flu.

Just look for the good things
That you can find.
Then go up to the person
And say something kind.

"Your new dress sure looks fine."

"Thanks for the help with my books."

"I liked playing with you."

"I love how that looks!"

It just means you have noticed.
You have said something true.
Think how good you would feel
If they said it to you.
Compliments are important.
They make others feel proud
That what you noticed was good,
And you said it out loud.
It shows that you care,
Have a CAP on your head,
To keep in the cold words
And spread warmth instead.

Sometimes it's hard
To know what to say.
The words don't come easy.
You're stuck in a way.
It's time to remember,
No time for dismay,
The next letter you'll need
In my CAP is the A.

A is for ASK
A question or two,
To show you have interest
In what your friends do.
Ask them about problems,
Their hopes and their fears,

Pretty soon you'll be hearing
Their thoughts in your ears.
If you listen enough
And show that you care,
You will make a new friend,
Maybe even a spare!

A is also for ACT,
That's ACT like you care,
Even though you may think
That the feelings aren't there.
The good feelings come
When you stop acting glum,

And practice the kind words
From which friendships come.
Don't think you'll sound phony.
It's just that you're scared
To tell people you like them,
To find out if they care.

Sometimes your kind words
Will fall on deaf ears,
And someone you like
Will say, "Get out of here!"
Don't give up completely
Or think it's the end.
It often takes more than
One try to make friends.

But if you keep trying
And a person's not nice,
You may find that their friendship
Is not worth the price.
A person who's mean
Should not take up your time.
So make efforts elsewhere.
Good friends you WILL find!

People are different.
You can't please them all.
Just try to stay friendly.
Don't let your CAP fall.
If you don't stop the questions,
The compliments too,
People learn you will listen
And they'll come to you.
Wear the CAP with the A
In the middle that shouts:

"ASK

some

questions

whenever

the

words

won't

come

out!"

The next letter is P
And it doesn't mean pout.
It's something important,
Of that there's no doubt.
P means be POSITIVE.
Hope for the best.
If you look on the bright side,
You've passed a big test.

To be POSITIVE means
When your class has a test,
You say, "We'll all do fine
If we study our best."
If the test is too hard
And you make some mistakes,
Say, "I'll study more next time"
Not "That teacher stinks!"

When the rain starts to fall
While you're winning a game,
Say, "Tomorrow's a new day...
We'll do this again."
Don't act like a baby
Whose diaper is wet,

Or a small boy who's angry
And kicks at his pet.

No one likes a complainer
Or person who groans.
When you do that, your friends
Say they have to go home.
It's goodbye to pouting
Or starting to whine.
A good attitude helps you
In life to do fine.

When things don't come easy,
Just say to your friends,
"Let's come back tomorrow...
We'll try it again."
Now you're wearing the CAP,
Like the one on my head,
To keep in the cold words
And spread warmth instead.

I've now told you my story
And you've listened quite well.
I'll be gone soon to find
Other people to tell.
Since it's getting so late,
I have one more request.
It all has to do
With the last letter, S.
I'll give you this gift,
But please wear it with style.
With my best letter S,
CAP it off with a SMILE!

If it's easy to say,
But not easy to do,
Just think how you react
To a smile or two.
When you are gloomy
And not feeling right,
Think how a small smile
Stops your wanting to fight.

With the CAP on your head
And a smile on your face,
You'll find that the world
Is not such a bad place.
Use the CAP sitting there
On the top of your head
To keep in the cold words
And spread warmth instead.

This won't work in a minute
And not in a day,
But make it a habit
And friends soon will stay.
Say goodbye to the bad words
And bad feelings too.
Pretend for awhile
If that's all you can do.
Make CAPS a motto,
A word you can say,
To remind you of how
You can make friends today!

Although she has written over 50 articles and/or book chapters in the field of psychology, this is the author's first children's book. Since 1980, Dr. Robin Inwald has been the director of Hilson Research, Inc., a well-known psychological test publishing company.

She is the author of over 25 psychological tests, including the *Hilson Adolescent Profile*, the *Hilson Children's Personality Profile*, and the *Inwald Personality Inventory*. Several of her tests now are used throughout the United States and in different countries to evaluate children and to screen job applicants.

Dr. Inwald earned a bachelor's degree in theatre arts and English from Cornell University, a Ph.D. in psychology from Columbia University, and a Certificate in Fine Art from Parson's School of Design. She lives in Kew Gardens, New York with her husband and three children. In the summer, they spend time at Lake George, where she enjoys tennis, windsurfing, and sunsets.